The No More Night Mares

A Dream of Freedom

This book is dedicated to Buck, my first horse and one of the great loves of my life... Special thanks to my daughter Callan, who encouraged me to finish this story and who recommended Kim as our artist. Kim has made the legend come to life with honor, beauty and a sense of spirit.

I hope this book captures your heart and encourages you to find the magic of these four-legged animals for yourself.

Dawn Van Zant

In the swirling mists and shadows of light and time live
ancient memories, forgotten dreams, and legends.

This is the legend of the "Night Mares".

It begins with tiny Eohippus, the Dawn Horse, from whom
all horses descend, and unravels with the evolution of
modern Equus. A magical descendent was erased from
history and can only be found in the legends of the night.
If you look far beyond the Big Dipper, past Polaris to the
Pegasus Constellation, you will find these missing horses
shining brightly. The luminous mares of a once noble herd
prance across a blanket of black sky. They are the "Night
Mares", strong, wild and free! They dream of a time long ago
when the land was filled with wild horses thundering across
vast plains. Their stars light up wishes, for a day when they
will be able to run free with the herds below and bring the
legend and magic to life!

Eclipse's Pledge - The Stallion

In the untamed lands of a time long ago lived a noble, wild stallion. His shining coat was painted black and he had a long, tangled mane and tail that curled and danced magically in the wind. He was born on a night when the moon passed through the Earth's shadow. At that very moment fate sealed his name: Eclipse. The legend tells us that the moon itself shone brightly in his wild eyes.

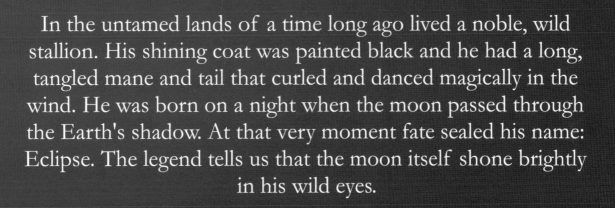

Eclipse was the fastest and strongest wild stallion in his territory. He kept his prized band of mares and foals well fed, safe, and hidden from danger. He led them past predators in the shadows of nightfall, guided safely by the moon and the stars. In the light of day their thundering hooves and clouds challenged even the fastest of winds. Nothing could catch them by night or by day.

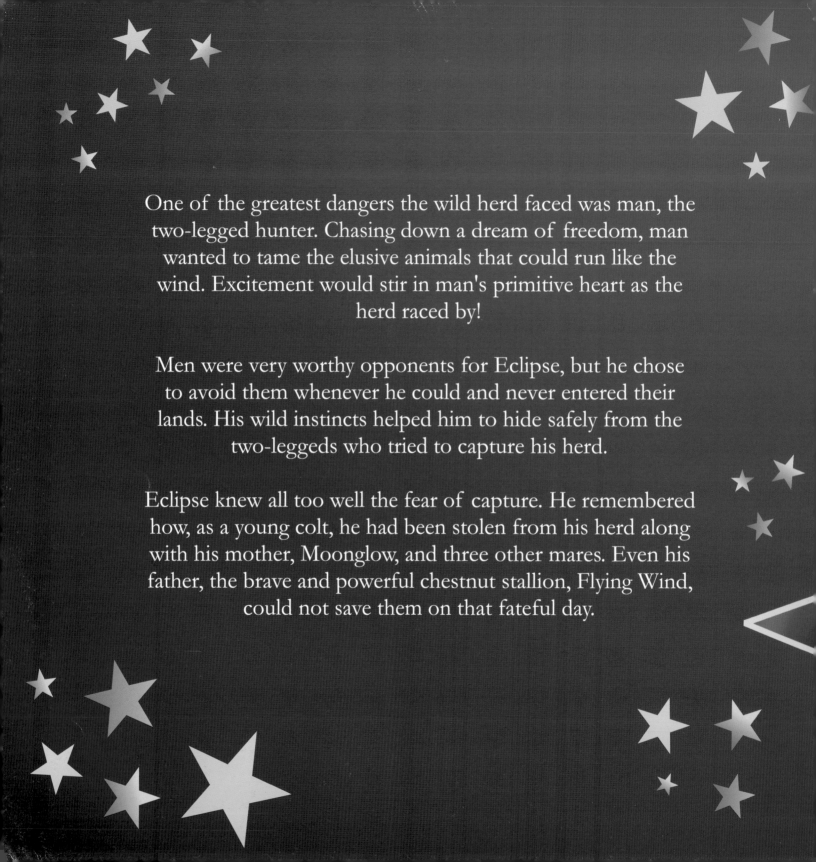

One of the greatest dangers the wild herd faced was man, the two-legged hunter. Chasing down a dream of freedom, man wanted to tame the elusive animals that could run like the wind. Excitement would stir in man's primitive heart as the herd raced by!

Men were very worthy opponents for Eclipse, but he chose to avoid them whenever he could and never entered their lands. His wild instincts helped him to hide safely from the two-leggeds who tried to capture his herd.

Eclipse knew all too well the fear of capture. He remembered how, as a young colt, he had been stolen from his herd along with his mother, Moonglow, and three other mares. Even his father, the brave and powerful chestnut stallion, Flying Wind, could not save them on that fateful day.

After many days and many months had slipped by under the light of the moon, Flying Wind finally found his beloved lost herd. He found them in small, fenced fields, where their memories of days with the wild herd were slowly fading away. Moonglow, his misty white mare, was losing her defiant lightning spirit. He whinnied and pounded the ground, calling to their wild hearts. As evening fell and the stars and the moon filled the sky, Eclipse heard the voice of freedom whispering to him in the evening breeze. He called to the mighty stallion Flying Wind, his mane rose, and his tail arched as though he was carrying a banner. He galloped to the wooden fence and struck the railings until they split and tumbled down beneath him. Eclipse and the mares were free once again! Straight away they ran swiftly towards their distant herd, in a gallop of victory.

In the days and weeks that followed, Flying Wind taught everything he knew to Eclipse. He believed that one day Eclipse would need to replace him as a great stallion. Eclipse promised the aging horse that he would never forget their fight for freedom. The two stallions reared and whinnied their pledge to the wind and sky above them.

Eclipse listened and watched, while he played stallion games, to learn from the mighty stallion. Flying Wind was a wise and gentle teacher, with the eye of a horse that had seen many things. In time, Eclipse began to follow his own instincts and found his path as a leader of the herd. In this way, he fulfilled the legacy of his father: to pass on what he knew.

Eclipse then asked the evening mist and the clouds to help hide and protect his herd. He knew that man never hunted the wild herds at night; he would pass through their lands under a blanket of darkness, leaving only a trail of silent hoofprints behind.

Eclipse's Herd

Eclipse had challenged another young stallion and won the most beautiful herd in his territory. He now had to guard his mares from the rogue stallions that envied his prize. He had his share of battle scars to prove his worth. His greatest challenger was the large, stocky buckskin named Golden Earth.

Golden Earth had a coat the color of willow, and a black mane and tail streaked with rays of sunshine. He had both wisdom and sorrow hidden in his large wide eyes that longed to tell his story. He was alone except for his reddish-brown mare, Earthquake, who was the last reminder of a once plentiful herd. When she galloped, her powerful hooves sent tremors across the land, with her long black tail and mane following like aftershocks in the air.

Every year Golden Earth galloped to the top of the hill to whinny and stomp, arching his strong neck. He snorted wildly until Eclipse would answer his war call. It was always an honourable fight, but one that never finished.

Golden Earth longed to have a herd of mares that was as beautiful as Eclipse's band. Although he knew they were not his mares, he felt the need to protect Eclipse's herd and watch over them, as a distant forgotten memory stirred beneath. He was always close by, as surely as the sun would rise.

A season of fresh green meadows, cool running waters, and warm weather came to Eclipse's herd during the year of his greatest challenge. There were nine mares and seven foals, which was a good-sized herd for a young stallion. It was a time of great pride for Eclipse. All of the foals were strong and bold just like their sire. Some were pintos, others were shades of black like him, while some were spotted and dappled.

His lead mare, Moonbeam, a pale and dusty palomino with a blaze that looked like a slice of the moon, had a foal named Moonshadow that looked just like Eclipse.

Moonshadow followed his mother everywhere, mimicking her every trot and canter perfectly. The small black shadow found his confidence by staying close to his mother, believing that one day he would be just as strong as his father, Eclipse.

Comet gave birth to a long-legged foal with a blaze that looked just like a streaking comet. The foal playfully followed the brown and white painted mare like a planet orbiting the sun.

Lucky Stars, a strong and gentle appaloosa with a spotted coat of stars sprinkled across her backside, quietly groomed and nuzzled her foal. The black stallion looked on ever so lovingly. When the herd thundered across the ground, it was a blur of flying manes, dancing tails and long legs! Golden Earth stood on a cliff and looked down at the herd and nickered softly as he admired this vision of beauty.

The Arrival of Man

Golden Earth searched across the land to find a pasture where he could graze quietly with his mare. He saw a small herd of strange animals moving slowly in the fields below his cliff-top. They walked on two legs and carried strange objects on their backs. At first he didn't know what they were, but his forgotten instincts pounded a dangerous warning beat to his heart. Then he saw something that filled him with fear and amazement.

He gazed curiously at two horses following behind the herd of these strange animals, carrying one on each of their backs. The animals' legs hung down around the horse's sides and they held onto their manes. The horses walked on quietly and calmly and did not resemble the wild horses he had seen only moments ago in Eclipse's herd. These were very different horses!

Golden Earth knew that the herd would return to graze in the pasture below where this new danger was awaiting them. The buckskin looked for another path down the mountain where he could go to warn Eclipse's herd. A rugged, steep trail offered a safe but slow descent.

Earthquake, his faithful mare, waited and stood guard on the hill above. Eclipse was alert and had keen eyesight, but Golden Earth knew that even his mighty opponent could not sense what was hiding in the long grass. Eclipse had to be warned of the pending danger.

Golden Earth walked through the field as quietly as a soft wind towards the herd in the distance. The lone stallion went by unnoticed. Earthquake still stood her ground.

The hunters waited to capture the mysterious horses that ran through the night like lightning in the sky. This herd had magical power. The men believed that if they rode on the backs of these horses the moon and the stars would protect them as well.

Once out of reach, Golden Earth galloped off to warn Eclipse of the danger. He ran faster than he ever had, covered in sweat, his heart pounding in his chest.

Eclipse heard Golden Earth's large hooves pounding the ground ahead of him. Golden Earth whinnied a loud warning that was carried on the wind to the herd. With his ears laid back, Eclipse put his nose to the wind and smelled the scent of man on Golden Earth's breath. His senses were flooded with the memories of his capture as a foal!

Freedom meant more than territory today! On this day, the two mighty stallions united to save the wild herd from the capture of man. Golden Earth gathered the foals and the slowest of the mares, while Eclipse called Moonbeam, Comet, and Lucky Stars (his fastest mares), to his side. With Eclipse leading them, they could outrun the men on their tame horses. Golden Earth helped to guide the rest of the herd to safer ground, where they would wait for Eclipse and lead the mares to their return.

And so the chase began...

The Chase

Eclipse stood on his hind legs and whinnied his challenge to the men in the distance. He thundered towards them, followed by his three mares. Clouds of dust surrounded the four horses as they galloped past the would-be captors. The herd ran united as one with the beating rhythm of their hearts and hooves. The wind danced through their manes and tails and sang a song of freedom!

The two-legged hunters waited, and then galloped behind on their horses. Dust and dirt from the hooves ahead of them flew into their faces. Their horses carried them swiftly, following the pace of the wild stallion. A wild calling rushed through their tame blood as they chased the herd. It gave them a strength and speed that thrilled the men on their backs! The chase continued as daylight faded and the darkness came.

The spirits of the darkness called to Eclipse. He was tired and weak from pursuit. His will carried him forward when his legs wanted to stop. The hunters thought they would have his mares before the night was over. Luckily, the pace slowed as the darkness surrounded the men. They were uncertain of the ground below them. A heavy mist was starting to rise in their path. This was what Eclipse was waiting for, his chance to vanish into the night air!

Eclipse looked up into the sky and whinnied a haunting cry for help. His call was picked up by the fog and carried by the wind into the night. It found its way to the mist around the full moon that glowed above them. "Free...keep my mares free...wild and free..." it whispered to the moon and the stars.

The horses that carried the hunters heard the wild plea. They felt the sorrow in the stallion's cry. They remembered their days of running free. They knew well what he was calling for, but they were from a very different world now. They had a new herd that included the two-leggeds. But like all of nature, they were still very wild at heart.

Spirits of Freedom

The forces of nature found in the moon and stars looked down on
the sweating and tired stallion, who would have run to the death to
save his herd. They looked ahead to the looming hills before the
wild horses and could see they were headed for the edge of a cliff.
The horses would be trapped with no place to run!

The sky spirits had always helped Eclipse, and they would again this
night, as the stallion led his herd through the darkness and fog.
The cold mist circled the moon and unravelled itself. It stretched
down to touch the cliff below. As Eclipse reached the edge and
faced his fear of capture, he heard a soft familiar whisper in the
wind. It was the spirit of Flying Wind calling from the past:

"A heart that is brave and true holds special magic.
Your call will be answered."

The magic of the moon and the stars in the sky spoke to him:
"Tell your mares to run. Let them keep running into the night mist
beyond the cliff and we will carry them up into the stars. They will
live safely in our sky, where man can only dream of them."

Eclipse whinnied to his mares to follow the path ahead
of them, and the mares galloped across the white mist that lay
like fresh snow, up and into the sky. Their hoof prints and
their echoing whinnies blazed a pathway to the stars.
It was magical and beautiful.

Guarding their escape, Eclipse turned to face the hunters.
The men stopped in fear and in awe. They were witnessing
magic too powerful to understand. They looked at the defiant
stallion whose eyes shone with the light of the moon.
They lowered their heads to him in respect. He was truly the
mightiest stallion in all the land. He could summon the magic
of the moon and stars with a valiant whinny!

The men turned their horses and slowly rode away from
the prized stallion. Tomorrow they would return to their
families and tell a tale of magic and power from which legends
would be made.

The stallion looked up into the sky above him and whinnied softly to his mares. Moonbeam, Comet and Lucky Stars twinkled back. He was filled with sadness and joy, knowing what he had won and lost that night. It was Eclipse's destiny to protect the herd on the earth below.

The Night Mares lit up the sky above him, showing him a safe path back to the herd that was waiting with Golden Earth. The radiant mares filled the sky with hope. The new stars in the galaxy shone rays of magic that filled the land below. Beams of light from their wild hearts travelled through space and time to ensure that the legacy of wild horses would not be forgotten.

He returned to his family and told them about the adventure of that mystical night. The horses bowed their heads in silence and vowed to pass on the legend and the legacy of their herd. Golden Earth whinnied goodbye to the herd and walked away towards his lone mare. Eclipse thanked his brave friend and knew in his wild heart that they were no longer foes. They would watch over their foals and their herd for generations to come.

Legend and Legacy

The Night Mares

A long time has passed since the days of Eclipse and his wild herd. The once plentiful wild herds have since vanished from the plains, now living as small scattered herds in refuge, or hiding in the outback. The history of wild horses alongside man has both defied and threatened their extinction. Man has been both a horse's best friend and his most brutal foe. But the legacy of man and horse continues…. as it always will. They gallop through our dreams to carry us to the stars. They stir the tamest imagination and comfort even the wildest hearts.

Night Mares look down upon us and watch over us. It's their dream that there will always be wild horses living on the land below as a reminder of freedom. We can chase them from the lands, but we can't reach them in the stars. So, if you awaken to a storm with lightning and thunder on a dark night, it may just be the Night Mares, streaking across the sky.

We don't have to be afraid of the dark...

Night Mares prance brilliantly against a background of
black sky and glowing stars to light our way to a time long
forgotten. Gaze up into their bright lights and they will
guide you through the darkest of nights. And if you
believe in them, they will fill you with a magical power.
Listen to the call of the wild herd and remember...

Comet...

faster than light

A comet racing across a black sky, its long tail shooting behind, filled the gentle eyes of Painted Sky as she gave birth to her foal.

The black and white mare nickered in pain and joy as she nuzzled her new baby and felt the newborn's breath upon her. Comet, her tiny brown and white painted foal, looked up and tried to see her admirer. Her big eyes filled with wonder as she saw the sky above filled with brilliant lights. Her imagination raced, and her small heart beat quickly to the rhythm of the new world she had entered.

Comet grew to live up to her birth name. As her body became larger and more powerful, she learned the thrill of her speed. She could run faster than light, with her long white tail streaking behind her. She raced the members of the herd and won over and over again. She challenged the fast flowing streams, the birds in the sky and the strongest winds. She loved the feeling of the wind filling her nostrils, dust and dirt flying in her two toned mane, and her hooves scorching the earth as she galloped across the land.

Comet can outrun anything that comes her way. Now that she is a Night Mare, she can gallop across the sky to rescue a wild horse below, or race the moonlight just for fun. If you believe in her, she will help you win the race of your life. Wish upon her star, and let her gallop into your heart.

Moonbeam...
a light of courage

On the night Moonbeam was born, the moon glimmered in the distance, shining softly on a mare and a foal. Moondance, the dark golden palomino licked her foal softly. Through the shadows of the night, she could see a white slice of moon on her foal's face. Moonbeam, the pale dusty palomino, stood up bravely and sniffed the night air.

She looked around at her new world with curiosity. The moonlight made her coat glisten. From the first day in the world she was a shining star in her mother's eyes. Her destiny was written in the sky: to become a Night Mare.

She played and ran with strength and courage as she grew. She showed the herd and the world that she had all the qualities of a lead mare. She would tease the other foals away from their mothers in hopes of discovering new adventures. She pawed the earth and stood her ground with any foal that dared to defy her. She would bite and chase them into her games. Unlike other foals, she never spooked at new sounds or sights. She chose instead to seek out their source.

As she grew into an adult mare, her beauty and courage were as apparent as a full moon on a clear night. Her soft eyes glowed with defiance in the face of danger. Eclipse whinnied to her for many moons after that fateful night, calling to her brave, wild heart in the distance. Her glistening silhouette ran with him on many dark nights, almost touching the earth with her thundering hooves. She is a source of light in a moment of darkness. If you believe in her, she will shine with rays of courage.

Lucky Stars...
lighting up smiles

Stardust filled the magical sky on the night that Lucky Stars was born. There was a sense of mischief in the air, as if pixies were at play sprinkling stardust on the coat of the newborn foal. Starlight, the appaloosa mare, knew that her foal was special as she tingled with the excitement of the new arrival. Lucky Stars took her first glance at the world and her eyes twinkled at her mother.

The mare watched in amusement as her baby tried to stand on her wobbly new legs. She fell over twice and then managed to stay up on her four long legs for a few moments. Her two back legs were stretched far apart, and she looked at her mother, almost smiling in the moonlight with her accomplishment.

The next morning, Lucky Stars was introduced to her father, the black and white spotted stallion named Galaxy. His big powerful neck stretched down to reach her and then arched to whinny in pride. Lucky Stars nickered and bucked and ran with excitement. Not having control over her body or her eyesight, she crashed into one of the older mares grazing in the herd. The young foal, confused, leapt back and ran to her mother's side. That was the beginning of a lifetime of playful mischief and accidents that made everyone around her, thank their "Lucky Stars".

As Lucky Stars grew to be a big powerful mare, her white appaloosa blanket sprinkled with strawberry roan stars became legendary. It was if she still had stardust on her back, spreading magic in the wind as she ran. Her eyes always twinkled with mischief. If you gaze up into the sky, look for a twinkling magical star. Lucky Stars will prance into your dreams and make your heart smile.